Mamá Goose

A LATINO NURSERY TREASURY
UN TESORO DE RIMAS INFANTILES

Alma Flor Ada and **F. Isabel Campoy**

Illustrated by **Maribel Suárez**

Creative editing of the English by Tracy Heffernan

HYPERION BOOKS FOR CHILDREN
NEW YORK

A Pablo García-Campoy
Que la alegría reflejada en estas palabras
sea tu más rica herencia.
Hope you will enjoy it in both languages!

A Colette Zubizarreta, capullito de alhelí
¡Bienvenida a la vida!
May you grow up to love your rich cultural heritage.

—F.I.C. and A.F.A.

First Edition
1 3 5 7 9 10 8 6 4 2
Printed in Singapore
Reinforced binding
Library of Congress Cataloging-in-Publication Data on file.
ISBN 0-7868-1953-7 (tr.)
Visit www.hyperionbooksforchildren.com

Índice

Contents

Introducción

Introduction

SPANISH is the third most widely spoken language in the world. It is spoken in nineteen countries in Latin America, in Spain, and by more than 40 million people in the United States. The vast and diverse geography and the multiple heritages that have contributed to the cultures of the Spanish-speaking people have created a folklore of extraordinary richness.

Spain, situated between Europe and Africa, with its extensive coastline, has always been a crossroads of civilizations. There, many cultures have coexisted and blended. Spanish folklore has been enriched by myths and stories of the Celts, who were the original inhabitants of the northwestern region; by the ancient traditions of the Basques; and by the Jewish and Arab presence for many centuries on the Iberian Peninsula.

When the Spanish crossed the Atlantic to settle in the Americas, they brought rhymes, songs, and medieval ballads that children often borrowed to accompany their games. Many of the traditional rhymes, sayings, songs, and lullabies changed and evolved to incorporate local elements. The Spanish treasury was enriched by the African people, who contributed their love for rhythm, musicality, and wordplay, as well as by the many indigenous peoples of the Americas.

What we offer in this book is a small sampler of this folklore. The pieces selected are well loved by many children, and most of them have a very wide distribution; thus they will be recognized by people of many different Spanish-speaking countries as part of their childhood experience. Because these pieces have been preserved orally, they have undergone transformation. Even in one country there may be several versions of some of the rhymes. Yet their essence remains intact. In the dynamic tradition of folklore, we have added our own original rhymes and poems, which introduce several sections of the book.

Offering these rhymes in Spanish is a way of recognizing their origins, and of inviting Spanish-speaking parents and grandparents to share their roots with new generations. Of course, for children who are learning Spanish, this book provides an opportunity to connect with the culture.

Offering the folklore in translation allows English-speaking children of any heritage to enjoy this timeless treasury.

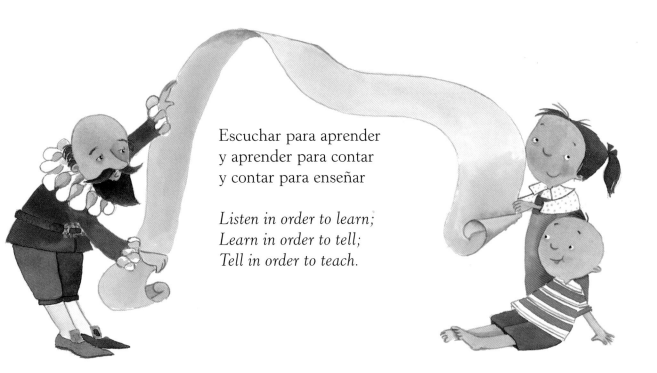

Escuchar para aprender
y aprender para contar
y contar para enseñar

Listen in order to learn;
Learn in order to tell;
Tell in order to teach.

Nanas
Lullabies

LULLABIES are known by many different names in the Spanish-speaking world: *nanas, arrullos, canciones de cuna, arrurrupatas*. But whatever the name, their goal is the same: to ease children into sleep, lulled by soft music and caring words.

Many lullabies repeat onomatopoeic sounds, inviting the young child to fall asleep: *arrorró* and *ea, ea, nanita* are both frequently part of such songs.

Hora de parar.

Hora de dormir.

Hora de cerrar los ojos

y guardar todos los sueños

dentro de ti

mientras te acurrucas para la noche.

Descansa el cuerpo y la cabeza,

sueña con todo lo que has leído.

En la mañana, al despertarte,

qué hermoso día el que crearemos.

Time to stop.

Time to sleep.

Time to close your eyes and keep

All sweet dreams

Inside your head,

While you slumber on your bed.

Rest your body, rest your head,

Dream of beautiful things we've read.

In the morning when you wake,

What a bright new day we'll make.

Esta niña linda

Esta niña linda
que nació de noche
quiere que la lleven
a pasear en coche.

Este niño lindo
que nació de día
quiere que lo lleven
a comer sandía.

Esta niña linda
no quiere dormir
quiere que la lleven
a ver el jardín.

Este niño lindo
no quiere dormir
cierra los ojitos
y los vuelve a abrir.

Estrellas de plata
luna de marfil
arrullen los niños
que van a dormir.

This Beautiful Girl

This beautiful girl,
Born in the night,
Wants to ride
In a carriage bright.

This beautiful boy,
Born in the sun,
Wants watermelon
For everyone.

This beautiful girl
Does not want to sleep.
A garden calls her
With flowers to keep.

This beautiful boy
Does not want to stop.
His eyes won't close,
They keep opening—pop!

Silver stars
Ivory moon
Sing them a song
With a sleepy tune.

4

La cuna de mi niño

Este niño mío
no tiene cuna
y las mariposas
le han hecho una.

La cuna de mi niña
se mece sola
como en el campo verde
las amapolas.

Duérmete, mi niño,
duérmete, ligero
que en su coche de oro
viene el lucero.

Duérmete, mi niña,
duerme sin pena
porque a tu lado siempre
tu madre vela.

Arrorró, mi niño,
toronjil de olor
duérmete a la sombra
de mi corazón.

My Child's Cradle

No cradle had
My little boy
Till the butterflies made one
Filled with joy.

My child's cradle
Rocks to and fro.
As waving red poppies
In the green field blow.

Go to sleep, sweet child,
Swiftly to rest.
The morning star comes
Dressed in its best.

Go to sleep, my child,
Rest without care.
Your mother watches
Your slumber fair.

Sleep, my sweet child,
The jasmine blooms
Within my heart
And in your room.

Din, don

Din, don; din, don, dan,
campanitas sonarán
que a los niños dormirán.

Duerme tranquilo, mi bien,
duermeté,
que yo tu sueño feliz,
guardaré.

Din, don; din, don, dan,
campanitas sonarán,
estrellitas brillarán
y los niños dormirán.

Ding-dong

Ding-dong, ding-dong,
Little bells will ring.
Children fall asleep
When the night bells sing.

Ding-dong, ding-dong,
Hear the bells' sweet song.
The stars shine above
While you sleep, my love.

Sweet dreams, my love,
I will watch over
And protect your dreams
While the moon beams.

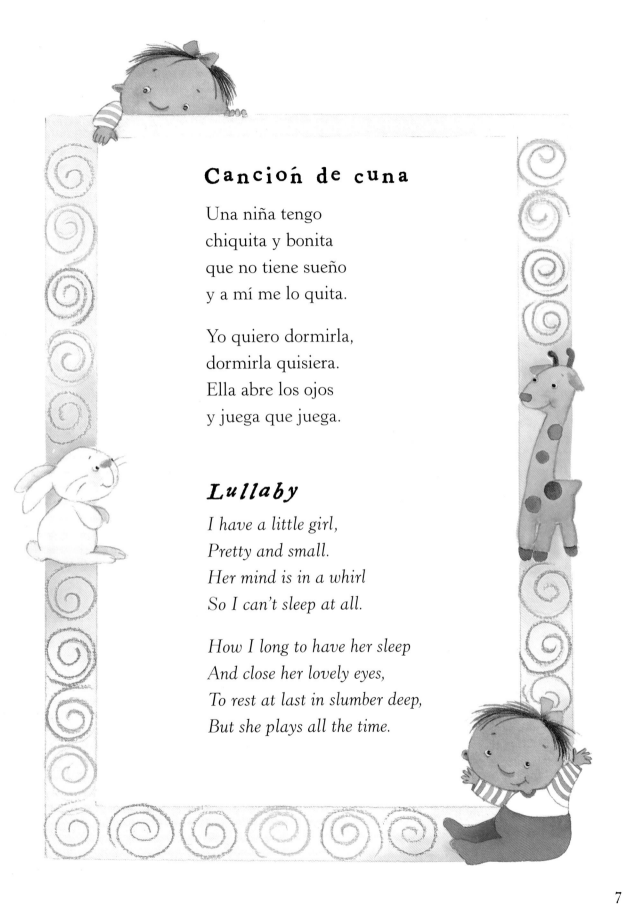

Canción de cuna

Una niña tengo
chiquita y bonita
que no tiene sueño
y a mí me lo quita.

Yo quiero dormirla,
dormirla quisiera.
Ella abre los ojos
y juega que juega.

Lullaby

I have a little girl,
Pretty and small.
Her mind is in a whirl
So I can't sleep at all.

How I long to have her sleep
And close her lovely eyes,
To rest at last in slumber deep,
But she plays all the time.

A la nana, nanita

A la nana, nanita,
nanita, ea.
A la cunita, madre,
que se menea.

Mereces cuna de oro
y no la tengo
pero tienes, tesoro,
todos mis besos.

A la nana, nanita,
que ya se duerme,
a la nanita, ea,
ya se durmió.

Sweet Dreams

Sweet dreams, little one,
Sweet dreams, my child.
The little cradle rocks
Slow and mild.

You deserve a golden cradle
Though I have none to give.
But I'll give you, my treasure,
Kisses as long as I live.

Sweet dreams, my child,
You're almost there.
To slumberland go
Without a care.

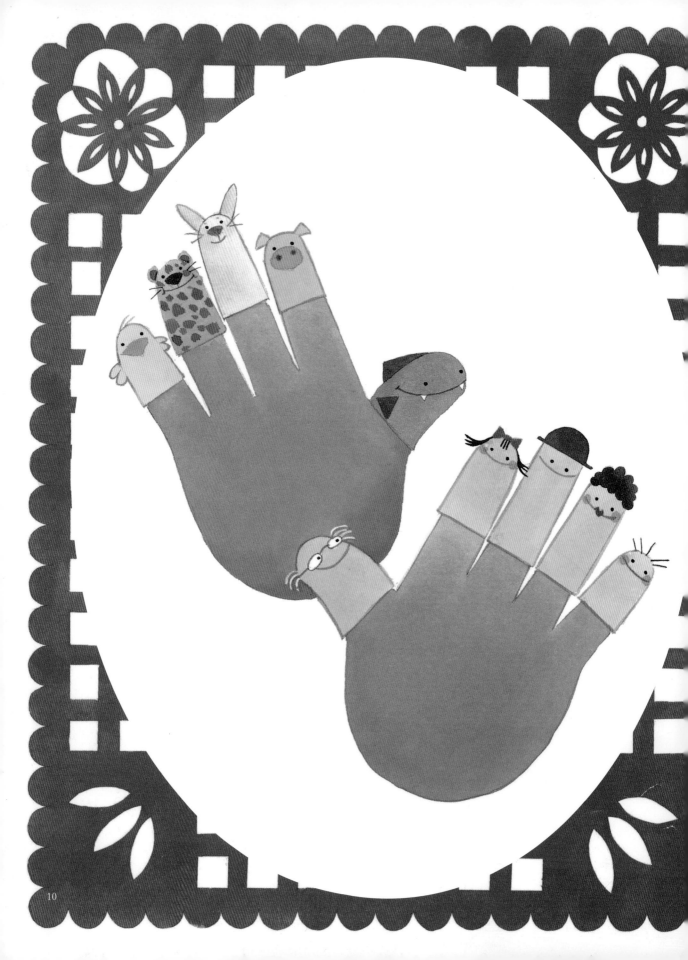

Juegos con los dedos
Finger Games

HANDS are a source of amazement for babies and toddlers. Finger games bring hand movements and words together in a way that allows a child to discover the integration of the body. *Juegos con los dedos* can be played by an individual child or a group, and no one is ever too old to enjoy them!

Cinco deditos
en una mano.
¡Cuántas cosas
pueden hacer!

¿Son una familia
siempre juntos?
¿Es la otra mano
un espejo mágico?

Five little fingers
All on one hand.
How many things
They can do!

Are they a family
Always together?
Is the other hand
A magic mirror?

Palmas y palmas

[dando palmadas]

Palmas y palmas,
higos y castañas,
almendras y turrón
para mi niño son.

Palmas, palmitas,
que viene papá
y trae un perrito
que dice guá, guá.

Clap, Clap

[clapping]

Clap, clap, clap,
Figs and chestnuts,
Almonds and nougat,
All for you.

Clap, clap, clap,
Here comes Daddy,
Bringing a puppy,
And he barks, too!

Doña Araña

[se imitan con las manos las acciones de la araña]

Doña Araña se fue a pasear
hizo un hilo y se puso a trepar,
vino el viento y la hizo bailar,
vino la tormenta y la hizo bajar.

Lady Spider

[imitating with hand movements the spider's actions]

Lady Spider spun a thread
To climb as high as the elephant's head.
Along came the wind, and made her dance.
Along came a storm, and she lost her chance.

Pececitos

[se mueven las manos para
imitar a dos pececitos nadando]

Riquirrín
y Riquirrán
son dos pececitos,
viven en el mar…

Son tan parecidos,
que no sé decir
cuál es Riquirrín
y cuál Riquirrán.

Little Fish

[moving both hands to
imitate fish swimming]

Riquirrán
And Riquirrín
Live in the sea
And swim, swim, swim.

They look so alike
I can never tell
Which is Riquirrín
And which is Riquirrán.

Pon, pon

[se une las puntas de los dedos y se golpea la palma
de la otra mano]

Pon, pon,

gallinita un huevo.

Pon, pon,

que no caiga al suelo.

Lay, Lay

*[knocking on the palm of one hand with the fingertips
of the other]*

Lay, lay

Your egg, Little Hen.

Lay it here.

Then lay it again.

Los cinco hermanitos

[se van señalando los cinco deditos, se comienza con el meñique y se acaba con el pulgar]

Éste compró un huevito,

éste lo partió,

éste lo cocinó,

éste le echó la sal,

y éste, pícaro gordo, se lo comió.

Five Little Brothers

[pointing to each finger, beginning with the pinky, ending with the thumb]

This little brother bought an egg,

This little brother made it crack,

This little brother cooked it up,

This little brother salts its back,

And this chubby brother went gobble, gobble, gobble

Till it was all gone.

Dos palomitas

[se mueven las manos para imitar a dos palomitas volando]

Dos palomitas en un palomar
la una se fue, la otra también.
Dos palomitas en un palomar
una volvió, la otra también.

Two Doves

[moving both hands to imitate the doves' flight]

Two little doves, next to each other.
One flew away, and then the other.
Two little doves, high in the sky.
One flew back home,
Then the other by and by.

19

Juegos en el regazo

Lap Games

YOUNG CHILDREN love to go exploring in an endless discovery of the world. But how wonderful to know there is a lap to welcome you back, where you can sit and rest . . . or jump and bounce.

Cómo me gusta estar en tu regazo, Mamá.
Ya que no me puedo quedar aquí para siempre
¿puedo saltar y mecerme un poquito?

How sweet to be in your lap, Mother.
Since I can't stay here forever,
Can I bounce and rock a little?

Los caballitos

[se mece al niño en las rodillas
  como si trotara en un caballo]

De los caballitos
que vienen y van
ninguno me gusta
como el alazán.

De cuatro caballos
que me han regalado
a mí el que me gusta
es el colorado.

De esos caballos
que vende usted
ninguno me gusta
como el que se fue.

Young Colts

[bouncing the child up and down
  on the knees, as if riding a horse]

Of all the little horses
Here and there
My very favorite
Is the chestnut mare.

Of the four horses
Given to me
My very favorite
Is the red pony.

Of all those horses
For sale today
My very favorite
Just ran away.

Al paso, al paso, al paso

[El adulto sienta al niño en una rodilla. El movimiento de la pierna aumenta con las palabras de la rima.]

Al paso, al paso, al paso,

al trote, al trote, al trote,

al galope, al galope, al galope.

Hop, Hop, Hop

[The adult has the child sitting on one knee.
The movement increases with the words of the rhyme.]

Walk, walk, walk.

Trot, trot, trot.

Gallop, gallop, gallop!

Arre, borriquito

[El niño, agarrado de ambas manos del adulto, cabalga sobre su rodilla.

Arre, borriquito,
vamos a Sanlúcar.
A comer las peras
que están como azúcar.

Arre, borriquito,
vamos a Jerez.
A comer las peras
que están como miel.

Arre, borriquito,
borriquito, arre.
Arre, borriquito,
que llegamos tarde.

So, so, so,
que ya se llegó.

Run, My Little Donkey

[The child, holding an adult's hands, rides upon the adult's knee.]

Run, my little donkey,
to Sanlúcar we go.
We will eat pears
Sugar-sweet and slow.

Run, my little donkey,
To Jerez for a treat.
We will eat pears
That taste honey-sweet.

Run, my little donkey,
Run, run, run.
Run, my little donkey,
Don't be late for fun!

Stop, stop, stop. Not so fast.
Here we are, here at last!

Dichos

Sayings

for Various Occasions

Para curar el dolor de un golpe

[La madre besa allí donde el niño se ha golpeado.]

Cura, sana,
madre rana,
dame un besito
y vete a la cama.

To fix a boo-boo

[The mother kisses where the child is hurt.]

Kiss, kiss,
Mother Toad,
Send the pain
Down the road.

Para preguntar la edad

Manzanita del Perú
¿cuántos años tienes tú?

To ask how old someone is

Little apple from Perú,
Tell me now, how old are you?

Cuando se encuentra una cosa

Una cosa me he encontrado
siete veces lo diré.
Si su dueño no aparece
con ella me quedaré.

When someone finds something

I have found something.
I say it seven times.
If no one claims it
Then it is mine!

Para encontrar algo perdido en el juego

—¿Qué has perdido?

—Una aguja y un dedal.

—Da tres vueltecitas
y lo encontrarás.

To find something that is lost during a game

—*What have you lost?*

—*A needle and a pin.*

—*Run around three times*
and then you will win!

Para indicar que uno se está divirtiendo

Del cielo cayó una palma,
del techo un melocotón,
entones dijeron todos:
—¡Que viva la reunión!

To show that you are having fun

A peach fell from the ceiling,
A palm fell from the sky,
Now sing out all together:
"What a wonderful time!"

Cuando alguien abandona un lugar y otro lo quiere ocupar

Quien fue a Sevilla
perdió su silla.

When someone leaves their place and someone else wants to occupy it

*You went to town
So I sat down!*

Cuando alguien quiere recuperar su lugar

Y quien fue y volvió
muy pronto se lo quitó.

When someone wants their place back

*I'm back from town—
Let me sit down!*

Rimas y canciones

Nursery Rhymes

POETRY is a child's lifelong friend. Nursery rhymes are repeated for the joy of the sound, rhythm, alliteration, and surprise. Later, as life's adventures unfold, these rhymes bring memories of carefree days.

Latino folklore is rich in rhymes and songs for all occasions. Many are about animals and play; others incorporate well-loved story characters. Some are nonsensical, while others invite reflection. All entertain and delight.

Las palabras	*Words*
se reúnen para jugar	*get together to play.*
saltan la cuerda,	*They skip rope,*
brincan y corren,	*hop, jump, and run.*
forman rimas	*They form rhymes*
y marcan el ritmo.	*and mark the rhythm.*
Las palabras	*Words*
cantan mientras juegan	*sing as they play*
y la vida	*and all life*
se vuelve canción.	*becomes a song.*

Debajo de un botón

Debajo de un botón, ton, ton,
que encontró Martín, tin, tin,
había un ratón, ton, ton.
¡Ay! qué chiquitín, tin, tin.

Under a Button

Under a button, button, button,
In Martin's house, house, house,
He found a tiny, tiny, tiny,
Hidden mouse, mouse, mouse.

El conejito

Entre los surcos
de los maizales
un conejito
corriendo va
y con sus brincos
siempre demuestra
cómo le gusta
la libertad.

A Little Bunny

A little bunny runs between
Rows of corn,
Hopping along as free
As the day he was born.

35

Cinco gatitos

Cinco gatitos
tuvo una gata,
cinco gatitos
detrás de una lata.
Cinco que tuvo,
cinco que criaba
y a todos cinco
lechita les daba.

Five Little Kittens

A cat had five kittens
Hiding behind the barn.
Five she had,
Five she raised,
Her milk kept them fed and warm.

Las once y media

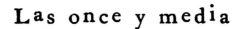

Las once y media serían
cuando sentí ruido en casa
bajo corriendo y, ¡qué veo!
que se paseaba una araña.
Lleno de furia y valor
saco mi luciente espada
y al primer tajo que doy
cae al suelo desmayada.
¡Qué cosa tan prodigiosa!
¿Vuelvo otra vez a contarla?

Eleven-Thirty

About eleven-thirty
I heard a noise downstairs.
I hurried off to see
a sight without compare!
A spider strolling around
With courage and with verve.
I took out my shining sword
And she lost her nerve.
She fainted and fell then—
Shall I tell it over again?

La guitarrita

Esta guitarrita mía
tiene lengua y quiere hablar,
sólo le faltan los ojos
para ponerse a llorar.

Los gallos cantan al alba,
yo canto al atardecer.
Ellos cantan porque saben
yo canto para aprender.

The Little Guitar

My little guitar
Has a tongue, but no eyes.
It wants to speak
And be able to cry.

Roosters sing at break of day,
At sunset I begin to play.
Roosters sing because they know how,
I sing to learn more than I know now.

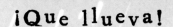

¡Que llueva!

Que llueva, que llueva,
la vieja está en la cueva.
Los pajaritos cantan,
las nubes se levantan.
¡Que sí! ¡Que no!
¡Que caiga un chaparrón!

Let It Rain

Let it rain! Let it rain!
The old woman must use her cane.
The little birds are all singing.
Rain is what the clouds are bringing.
Oh yes! Oh no!
Here comes the downpour!

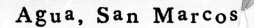

Agua, San Marcos — *Water, Saint Marcus*

Agua, San Marcos,	*Water, Saint Marcus,*
rey de los charcos,	*The puddle king,*
para mi triguito	*My wheat needs*
que está muy bonito;	*The rain you bring.*
para mi cebada,	*Water my barley*
que ya está granada;	*That is all grown,*
para mi melón,	*And the honeydew*
que ya tiene flor;	*All my own;*
para mi sandía,	*For my watermelon*
que ya está florida;	*In full bloom,*
para mi aceituna,	*And my olive tree*
que ya tiene una.	*With fruit coming soon.*

41

Comadrita, la rana

[Los niños cantan esta canción, en cuclillas,
saltando como ranas.]

—Comadrita, la rana.

—Señor, señor.

—¿Llegó su maridito del bosque?

—Sí, señor.

—Y, ¿qué le trajo?

—Un mantón.

—¿De qué color?

—Verde limón.

Sapito y pon,

sapito y pon.

Lady Frog, My Friend

*[Children sing this song facing each other
while jumping like frogs.]*

—Lady Frog, my friend.

—Sir, yes, sir?

—Has your husband returned home?

—Sir, yes, sir!

—What did he bring you?

—An embroidered shawl.

—What color was it?

—Lemon green—that's all.

Little toad, little toad,
Pollywog-wog.

La Hormiguita y Ratón Pérez

La Hormiguita y Ratón Pérez
se casaron anteayer.
¿Dónde fue? Yo no lo sé.
Que coloretín, que coloretón.
¡Que viva la Hormiga,
que viva el Ratón!

Ella es buena y hacendosa,
él es muy trabajador.
Que coloretín, que coloretón.
¡Que viva la Hormiga,
que viva el Ratón!

The Little Ant and Pérez the Mouse

Pérez the Mouse and the little Ant
Got married on Tuesday.
Can you tell where? I can't.
May they have a long and colorful life!
Long live the Mouse and his little Ant wife!

She is creative and so good.
He is hardworking,
Knock on wood.
May they have a long and colorful life!
Long live the Mouse and his little Ant wife!

Canciones de comba

Jump-Rope Songs

JUMPING ROPE is a favorite game in Spanish-speaking countries. Ropes may be new and colorful or old and frayed, but all provide the pretext for jumping and following the rhythm of ancient and modern rhymes.

Mediodía
en el patio de la escuela
las niñas
se reúnen a jugar.
Dos sostienen la cuerda
una salta dentro
y las tres mantienen
el mismo compás.

Tarde en la tarde
de verano
en la plaza del pueblo
se reúnen los amigos.
Cada uno tiene una cuerda
cada uno, una canción
todo saltan muy alto
al mismo son.

Midday
In the school yard,
Young girls
Meet to play.
Two hold the rope,
One jumps inside
keeping the rhythm.
All sing at once.

Late afternoon
On a summer day
In the town plaza
The friends gather.
Each has a rope,
Each has a song,
Up in the air
All jump along.

A la una canta el gallo

A la una canta el gallo,
a las dos la totovía,
a las tres el ruiseñor
y a las cuatro ya es de día.

The Rooster

The rooster crows at one,
The songbird sings at two,
At three the nightingale,
At four the day is new.

Caballito blanco, reblanco

Caballito blanco,
reblanco,
sácame de aquí,
llévame hasta el puerto
donde yo nací.

Little White Horse

Little horse
White as snow
Take me where
I long to go.
Take me to the port
By the sea
Where I was born
And long to be.

49

Pluma, tintero y papel

Una, dos y tres,
pluma, tintero y papel
para escribir una carta
a mi querido Miguel.

Paper, Ink, and Pen

One, two, three,
paper, ink, and pen,
all to write a love letter
to my sweetheart, Ben.

Soy la reina de los mares

Soy la reina de los mares
y ustedes lo van a ver,
tiro mi pañuelo al suelo
y lo vuelvo a recoger.

Pañuelito, pañuelito,
quién te pudiera tener
guardadito en el bolsillo
como un pliego de papel.

The Queen of All Oceans

I'm the queen of all oceans.
You will see why when
I throw my hankie to the floor
And pick it up again.

My precious little hankie,
I'd like to keep you here,
Folded like paper
In my pocket, always near.

La carbonerita

En Salamanca tengo,
ten, ten, ten,
tengo sembrado
azúcar y canela,
pi, pi, pi
pimienta y clavo.

¿Cómo quieres que tenga,
la, la, la,
la cara limpia,
si soy carbonerita
de, de, de
de Salamanca?

The Coal-seller

In Salamanca
I have, have, have
Fields of sugar, cinnamon,
Pep-pep-pepper, and clove.

How, you ask
As I roll, roll, roll,
Can I keep my face clean,
Sell-sell-selling black coal?

53

El paseíto de oro

El paseíto de oro
es muy bonito,
por donde se pasean
los señoritos.

Las señoritas llevan
en la sombrilla
un letrero que dice:
¡Viva Sevilla!

Los señoritos llevan
en la cartera
un letrero que dice:
¡Viva la escuela!

The Golden Path

The golden path
Is lovely here,
The young gents walk
Its pathway clear.

The young girls
Carry parasols
Proclaiming "Seville
Is the greatest of all!"

The young boys
Have a sign too.
Their backpacks say:
"Long live the school!"

Canciones de ronda

Song Games

SONGS may accompany games or even be the pretext for a game. Some of the songs Spanish-speaking children sing today are very ancient, and some are remnants of medieval ballads.

¡Cantemos!	*Let's sing!*
¡Juguemos!	*Let's play!*
¡Cantemos y juguemos!	*Let's sing and play!*

La viudita del Conde Laurel

—Doncella del prado
que al campo salís
a coger las flores
de mayo y abril.

—Yo soy la viudita
del Conde Laurel
que quiere casarse
y no encuentra con quien.

—Pues siendo tan bella
no encuentras con quien,
escoge a tu gusto
que aquí tienes cien.

—Yo escojo a esta niña
por ser la primera,
por ser la más bella
de todo el jardín.

—Y ahora que hallaste
la prenda querida
contenta a su lado
pasarás la vida.

58

Gathering the Flowers

"Young lady
Walking in the fields
Gathering the flowers
That May and April yield."

"I am the widow
Of Count Laurel.
I would like to marry,
But whom, I cannot tell."

"You are so beautiful,
You may have your pick.
A hundred would say yes
And never resist."

"I choose this one,
The first one I've seen,
And the most gentle
In this lovely garden."

"And now that you've found
The partner you request,
Happily you'll live
Side-by-side and blessed."

Juguemos en el bosque

[Uno los niños, que está escondido, es el lobo.
Los demás niños cantan preguntándole si está.
El lobo responde enumerando cada vez las distintas prendas de vestir hasta que dice los zapatos
que es la señal para salir a perseguirlos. El niño a
quien agarre sera el próximo lobo.]

—Juguemos en el bosque mientras
el lobo no está. Lobo, ¿estás?

—Me estoy poniendo los pantalones.

—Juguemos en el bosque mientras
el lobo no está. Lobo, ¿estás?

—Me estoy poniendo la camisa. . . .

—Me estoy poniendo la corbata. . . .

—Me estoy poniendo los calcetines. . . .

—Me estoy poniendo los zapatos. . . .

60

Let's Play in the Woods

[*One child, in hiding, is the wolf. The rest of the children keep singing and the wolf keeps answering until he says he's putting on his shoes—the signal to chase the others. The child the wolf catches is the next wolf.*]

"Let's play in the woods
While the wolf's away.
Wolf, Wolf, where are you?
Can we safely play?"

"I'm putting on my pants."

"Let's play in the woods
While the wolf's away.
Wolf, wolf, where are you?
Can we safely play?"

"I'm putting on my shirt. . . .

"I'm putting on my tie. . . .

"I'm putting on my socks. . . .

"I'm putting on my shoes. . . .

Antón Pirulero

[Mientras los niños cantan el que hace de Antón Pirulero hace como si tocara distintos instrumentos: el piano, la guitarra, el acordeón, la trompeta. . . . los demás deben imitar sus movimientos. Si alguno se equivoca debe entregar una prenda. Para recuperar las prendas, sus dueños deberán cumplir los castigos que los demás le impongan: saltar en un pie, pararse de cabeza, decir un chiste, etc.]

Antón, Antón,
Antón Pirulero,
cada cual, cada cual
atienda a su juego.
Y el que no lo atienda,
pagará, pagará,
pagará una prenda.

Antón, Antón …

Antón Pirulero

[*While singing the song, the leader does hand movements as if playing a specific instrument: piano, violin, guitar, accordion, etc. Everyone must follow closely with the same movements. If someone fails to do so, that person will have to give a token. Later, to retrieve the token, the person will have to do whatever he or she is asked to do: jump on one foot, stand on his head, tell a joke, etc.*]

Antón, Antón,
Antón Pirulero,
Everyone is watching
To see what moves to make,
And from the one who gets it wrong,
A token we will take.

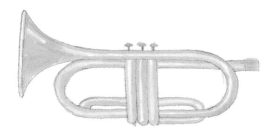

Antón, Antón. . . .

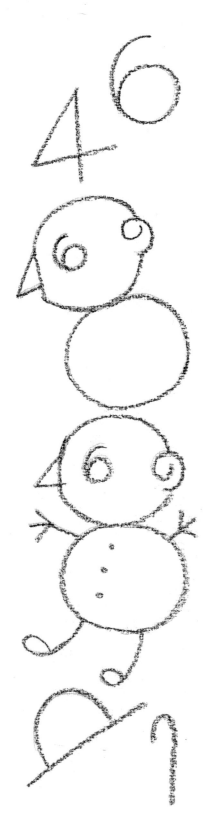

Dibujando un garabato

Con un seis y un cuatro,
aquí tienes tu retrato.

Luego traza con destreza
la curva de la cabeza.

Si adentro pintas un nueve,
la oreja a salir se atreve.

Una curva a cada lado
y el cuerpo ya está pintado.

Y sin muchas desazones
le ponemos tres botones.

Las piernas y los zapatos
se hacen con dos garabatos.

Con dos rayas y palitos
aquí tienes los bracitos.

Una raya y medio cero,
y ya tienes el sombrero.

Y con una raya más
hasta tu bastón tendrás.

Pues con bastón y sombrero
eres todo un caballero.

64

Doodles

Write six above four—you've begun
To draw your portrait, just for fun.

Now link them with a curved line
To make the head, round and fine.

Put the number nine right here—
Now you see a little ear.

Draw a curve down each side;
Here your body will abide.

It's no trouble at all, you know,
To draw three buttons in a row.

With a couple of scribbles—one, two—
You will have the legs and shoes.

Add two long lines and short ones, please,
To make the arms and legs with ease.

A line with a half circle above
Creates a hat that you'll just love.

And with just one more line here
A cane will magically appear.

Now, with a cane and a hat
You are a gentleman, imagine that!

Lunes antes de almorzar

Lunes antes de almorzar
a una niña fui a buscar
pero no podía jugar
porque tenía que trabajar.
    Así lavaba, así, así,
    así lavaba, así, así,
    así lavaba, así, así,
    así lavaba que yo la ví.

Martes antes de almorzar
a una niña fui a buscar
pero no podía jugar
porque tenía que trabajar.
    Así planchaba, así, así,
    así planchaba, así, así,
    así planchaba, así, así,
    así planchaba que yo la ví.

Miércoles antes de almorzar. . .
    Así cocinaba, así, así . . .

Jueves antes de almorzar . . .
    Así fregaba, así, así . . .

Viernes antes de almorzar . . .
    Así cosía, así, así . . .

Sábado antes de almorzar . . .
    Así barría, así, así . . .

Domingo antes de almorzar
a una niña fui a buscar
¡Ahora sí podía jugar,
ya no había que trabajar!

Before Lunch on Monday

Before lunch on Monday
I looked for a girl to play,
But she could only work and slave
All the livelong day.
This is how she washed:
    like this, like this, like this.

Before lunch on Tuesday
I looked for a girl to play
But she could only work and slave
All the livelong day.
This is how she ironed:
    like this, like this, like this.

Before lunch on Wednesday . . .
This is how she cooked . . .

Before lunch on Thursday . . .
This is how she cleaned . . .

Before lunch on Friday . . .
This is how she sewed . . .

Before lunch on Saturday . . .
This is how she swept . . .

Before lunch on Sunday
I looked for a girl to play.

And she finally said:
"No work today!"

Refranes
Proverbs

PROVERBS are a part of many cultures. These pearls of wisdom convey messages gleaned from life experience in just a few words or a metaphor.

While in some cultures proverbs may seem somewhat old-fashioned and their use may be in decline, throughout the Spanish-speaking world these expressions of popular wisdom continue to be much used. In Spanish, a clear distinction is made between *proverbios*, those sentences taken from the Bible or other literary sources, and *refranes*, which derive from popular wisdom.

Latinos in the United States have diverse countries of origin and varied life experiences, but if one says "*Dime con quién andas...*" (Tell me who your friend is . . .), all of them, regardless of their ancestry or status, will be able to respond "*y te diré quién eres*" (and I'll tell you who you are).

Breves palabras	*A few words*
que dicen mucho.	*That tell you much,*
Nos dan consejo	*Give you advice,*
y apoyo.	*And support too.*
Úsalas con afecto	*Use them wisely*
cuídalas de verdad	*For they hold*
porque su sabiduría	*Great wisdom*
no tiene edad.	*For young and old.*

Dime con quien andas y te diré quién eres.
Tell me who your friend is, and I will tell you who you are.

Haz bien y no mires a quién.
Do good to others, no matter who they are.

El haragán trabaja doble.
The lazy person will work twice as much.

De tal palo, tal astilla.
The chip resembles the block.

No se ha de exprimir tanto la naranja, que amargue el zumo.
Squeezing it too much makes the orange give bitter juice.

La avaricia rompe el saco.
Greed breaks the bag.

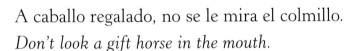

A caballo regalado, no se le mira el colmillo.
Don't look a gift horse in the mouth.

A buen hambre no hay pan duro.
Hunger makes a stale loaf fresh again.

Adivinanzas

Riddles

Adivina, adivinador.	*Riddler, answer the riddle.*
Adivina, adivinanza.	*Riddle upon riddle.*
¿Que será, qué podrá ser?	*What is it? What can it be?*
¿Qué será, que sería/que en mi casa no lo había?	*What is it? What could it be?* *It was not in my house.*

UPON HEARING any of these calls, Spanish-speaking children know a riddle will follow.

Some traditional riddles in Spanish may be based on linguistic clues. The sounds of words in the riddle may hold the answer. For example: "Oro parece, *plata no* es." In English, "It looks like gold, it is not silver" does not provide much of a clue. But in Spanish, the answer to the riddle, *plátano* (banana) is hidden in the words of the riddle: *plata no*.

Other riddles do not depend on linguistic features and contain different types of clues. Traditional riddles tend to be two lines of six, seven, or eight syllables. But whatever the structure, they will make you think and laugh.

¿Qué será?	*What is it?*
¿Qué podrá ser?	*What can it be?*
Escucha con cuidado	*Listen carefully*
y luego . . . pensarás.	*Then . . . think.*
La respuesta está cerca	*The answer is clear,*
la respuesta está aquí	*The answer is near.*
ya vas a descubrirla . . .	*You can discover it . . .*
¡claro que sí!	*It is right here!*

¿Qué cosa va siempre
detrás del ratón?   [La cola]

What always
follows a mouse?   *[Its tail]*

¿Quién es el que camina
y lleva su rancho encima?   [El caracol]

Who travels far
but never leaves his house?   *[A snail]*

¿Qué es lo que no tiene pies y corre,
no tiene dedos y lleva anillos?   [La serpiente]

*Who can run without feet
and has rings, but no fingers?*   *[A snake]*

75

Camina con la cabeza
y no tiene pereza.   [La pelota]

Never stops, never lazy—
It bounces like crazy.   *[A ball]*

Ronda que ronda, rondadorita,
teje que teje, tejedorita.   [La araña]

This weaver weaves
round and round,
weaving, weaving
without a sound.   *[A spider]*

Vengo de padres cantores,
pero yo cantor no soy.
Tengo blanca la capita
y amarillo el corazón.   [El huevo]

I do not sing,
But my parents might.
I have a yellow heart
And a cape of white.   *[An egg]*

En noche clara
brillo en el cielo
rodeada de estrellas
y de luceros.   [La luna]

On a clear night
You can see me for miles.
The stars twinkle
And I smile.   *[The moon]*

A pesar de tener patas
no me sirven para andar
Tengo la comida encima
y no la puedo probar.   [La mesa]

I have legs, but they don't help me walk.
I serve food, but I cannot eat it.   *[A table]*

Verde como loro
bravo como toro.   [El chile verde]

Green as a parrot,
brave as a bull.   *[A green chili pepper]*

Mientras que estoy preso, existo,
si me liberan, muero.   [El secreto]

If you keep me,
I am here.
Once let out,
I disappear.   [A secret]

Tengo hojas sin ser árbol,
te hablo sin tener voz.
Si me abres no me quejo.
Adivina quién soy.   [El libro]

I have leaves, but am no tree.
I have no voice, yet I talk to you.
I won't complain when you open me.
If you guess who I am, I can walk with you!   [A book]

Una pregunta

—Ahora que estamos juntos
una pregunta le haré:
¿Cuántos pelos tiene un gato
acabado de nacer?

—De la pregunta que me hace
la respuesta le daré:
Si no ha perdido ninguno
todos los ha de tener.

A Question

—*Now that we're together,*
A question I will ask.
How many hairs has a newborn
  kitten?
Are you up to the task?

—*The answer is simple,*
It is safe to say,
It has all it was born with
If it has given none away.

Patrañas y cuentos de nunca acabar

Tall Tales and Never-Ending Stories

NEVER–ENDING STORIES and tall tales in verse are common in Latino folklore.

Un cuento que no se acaba
ya lo verás.
El final es el principio
y el principio es el final.
¿Quieres que te lo cuente otra vez?

What is a story that never ends?
The ending is the beginning,
And the beginning, the end.
Shall I tell it to you again?

Un cazador

Un cazador, cazando,
perdió el pañuelo
y después lo llevaba
la liebre al cuello.

El perro, al alcanzarla,
se lo arrebata
y con él se hace el nudo
de la corbata.

Al cazador, la liebre,
muerta de risa
le quita la escopeta
y la camisa.

El cazador se queda,
ay, qué pirueta
sin camisa, sin moño,
sin escopeta.

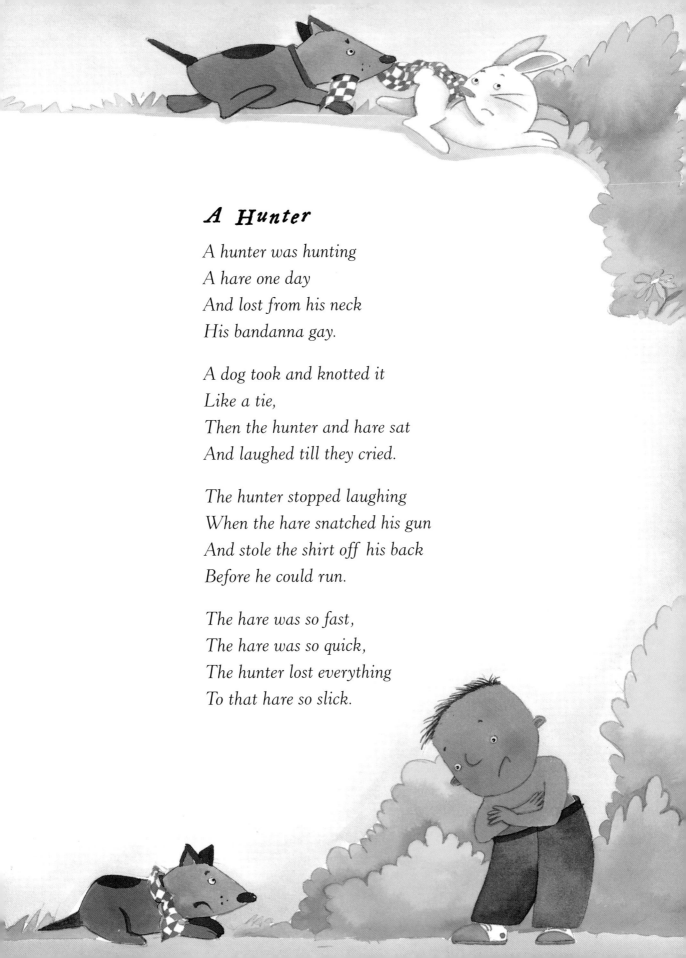

A Hunter

A hunter was hunting
A hare one day
And lost from his neck
His bandanna gay.

A dog took and knotted it
Like a tie,
Then the hunter and hare sat
And laughed till they cried.

The hunter stopped laughing
When the hare snatched his gun
And stole the shirt off his back
Before he could run.

The hare was so fast,
The hare was so quick,
The hunter lost everything
To that hare so slick.

La hormiguita

Ésta era una hormiguita
que de un hormiguero
salió calladita
y se metió a un granero,
se robó un triguito
y arrancó ligero.

Salió otra hormiguita
del mismo hormiguero
y muy calladita
se metió en el granero,
se robó un triguito
y arrancó ligero.

Salió otra hormiguita
del mismo hormiguero
y muy calladita
se metió en el granero,
se robó un triguito . . .

The Ant

Here comes the ant
Out of its hole,
Grabs a grain of wheat
And returns like a mole.

Another ant comes
Out of its hole,
Grabs a grain of wheat
And returns like a mole.

ANOTHER ant comes
Out of its hole . . .

La villa de Pardiez

En la villa de Pardiez
todo, todo es al revés:
los zapatos en las manos
y los guantes en los pies.

En la villa de Pardiez,
todo, todo es al revés:
cuando compran pagan cuatro,
cuando venden cobran tres.

En la villa de Pardiez,
todo, todo es al revés:
el ratón lo corre al gato
y el ladrón condena al juez.

En la villa de Pardiez,
todo, todo es al revés:
lo que ganan en un año
se lo gastan en un mes.

In Pardiez Town

In Pardiez town, in Pardiez town,
Everything is upside down.
Shoes on hands, gloves on feet,
Walking backward through the street!

In Pardiez town, in Pardiez town,
Everything is upside down.
When they buy, they pay for four,
But they're charged for three, no more!

In Pardiez town, in Pardiez town,
Everything is upside down.
Mice chase cats, without fail
And thieves put the judge in jail!

In Pardiez town, in Pardiez town,
Everything is upside down.
Twelve months they earn and save and save
To spend it all in thirty days!

89

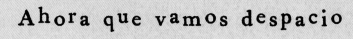

Ahora que vamos despacio

Ahora que vamos despacio
vamos a contar mentiras:
por el mar corren las liebres,
por el monte las sardinas.

Salí de mi campamento
con hambre de seis semanas,
al pasar vi un ciruelo
cargadito de manzanas;
empecé a tirarle piedras
y caían avellanas.

Con el ruido de las nueces
salió el amo del peral:
—Niño, no le tires piedras,
que no es mío el melonar.

90

Now That We Are Walking Slowly

Now that we are taking a stroll,
Let's tell some stories, tall and droll.
Hares come running from the sea,
Sardines swim the hills, tralee!

When I left the camp, I was so hungry.
Then I spied a laden apple tree!
At its branches I threw stones by the bunch,
And dozens of almonds dropped for my lunch.

The nuts made so much noise coming down,
The owner of the pear tree came around.
"Child," he said, "please, don't throw stones.
The melon fields are not my own!"

91

Un romance
A Ballad

HOW WONDERFUL to hear a whole story that can also be sung! That is what ballads are: long poems that tell a story and can be put to music.

The old medieval ballads that told of the adventures of knights, of love between princes and beautiful ladies, of the sadness of prisoners, or of the woman whose husband has gone to war, form the origins of today's popular *corridos*, songs about unrequited love and separations.

The ballad form occurs often in children's folklore. Here is one of the best-loved ballads for children.

El señor don Gato

Estaba el señor don Gato
en silla de oro sentado,
calzando medias de seda
y zapatitos dorados.

Nuevas le fueron venidas
que había de ser casado
con una gatita parda
hija de un gato romano.

El gato de puro gusto
subió a bailar al tejado,
mas le dieron con un palo
y rodando vino abajo.

Se ha roto siete costillas
y la puntita del rabo.
Ya llaman a los doctores,
sangrador y cirujano.

Unos le toman el pulso,
otros le auscultan el rabo.
Todos dicen a una voz:
—¡Muy malo está el señor Gato!

Tuvo que hacer testamento
por lo mucho que ha robado:
cuatro quesos, dos morcillas
y un chorizo muy salado.

A la mañana siguiente
amaneció muerto el gato.
Ya lo llevan a enterrar
por la calle del Pescado.

Las gatas se ponen luto;
los gatos, capotes pardos
y los gatitos chiquitos
lloraban desconsolados.

Los ratones, de contentos,
se visten ¡de colorado!
Al olor de las sardinas
el gato ha resucitado.
Los ratones corren, corren,
detrás de ellos corre el gato.

The Ballad of Sir Cat

Sir Cat was sitting
On his golden chair
Dressed in silk stockings
And gold shoes so fair.

News came, he must
Marry a calico lady,
Daughter of a Roman cat,
Whose name was Sadie.

Sir Cat was elated
And danced on the roof,
Till someone knocked him
   with a stick
Down to the street—POOF!

Seven ribs were broken
And the tip of his tail.
Doctors, nurses, surgeons
Were called, to no avail.

Some took his pulse,
Others listened by his tail.
All agreed at once,
"Sir Cat is quite ill!"

He had to write his will
For all the things he stole:
Four cheeses, two sausages,
Salty chorizo cold.

Next day he was gone,
Ready to be buried.
Through the streets of fish,
His body was carried.

Lady cats and gents came
All dressed in black.
Little kittens wiped their eyes,
Sad for Sir Cat.

The mice celebrated, of course,
And wore bright red.
But the smell of sardines
Woke him from the dead.

Once again the mice must run
For here comes Sir Cat.
The sardines brought him back to life
And that, my child, is that!

Canciones

Songs

IN LATINO CULTURES, the interweaving of African, Native American, and Spanish traditions has given birth to universally cherished musical forms and instruments. The guitar, for instance, was born in Spain.

The love for music begins very early among Latinos, and the repertoire of songs cherished by children is enormous. Here are just a few samples that have transcended time and distance to be commonly enjoyed by children throughout the Spanish-speaking world.

Pájaro en la rama,
agua en el río,
poema en la página,
palabras en mi corazón.
Toda la vida, una canción.

Birds on the branch,
Water in the river,
A poem on the page,
Words in my heart.
All life, a constant song.

Una paloma blanca

Una paloma blanca
que del cielo bajó
con las alas doradas
y el piquito de miel.
En el pico una rama
en la rama una flor
son las niñas bonitas
como rayos del sol.

A White Dove

From the sky
Came a white dove
With golden wings
And a beakful of honey.
Its beak held a branch,
On the branch, a blossom
Whose petals are
Pretty little girls
Like rays of the sun.

Una tarde fresquita de mayo

Una tarde
fresquita de mayo
me fui a pasear,
por la senda
donde mi morena,
morena graciosa,
solía pasar.

Yo la vi
coger una rosa.
Yo la vi
que admiraba un clavel.
Yo le dije:
—Jardinera hermosa,
si me das una rosa
yo te doy un clavel.

On an Afternoon in May

I went out walking
On a fresh May afternoon,
Down the path where I knew
My love would come soon.

I saw her pluck a rose,
For a carnation longing too.
And I said, "Fair gardener,
Give me that rose,
And this carnation I'll give to you."

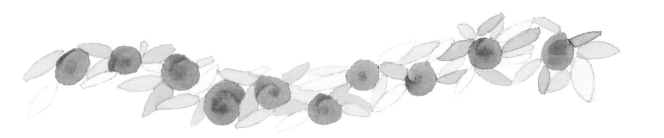

La Tarara	*Tarara*
Tiene mi Tarara	*My Tarara*
un vestido verde	*Has a green gown*
lleno de lunares	*With polka dots*
y de cascabeles.	*And jingle bells up and down.*
La Tarara sí,	*Tarara, yes,*
la Tarara, no,	*Tarara, no,*
la Tarara, niña,	*Tarara, yes, darling,*
que la bailo yo . . .	*Dancing we will go. . . .*
Tiene mi Tarara	*My Tarara*
un cesto de flores	*Has a basket of flowers.*
que si yo le pido	*If I ask her,*
me da las mejores.	*She gives me the prettiest for my bower.*
La Tarara sí,	*Tarara, yes,*
la Tarara, no,	*Tarara, no,*
la Tarara, niña,	*Tarara, yes, darling,*
que la bailo yo!	*Dancing we will go!*

Canciones de cumpleaños

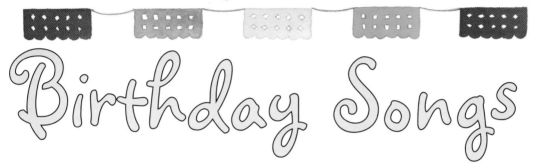

Birthday Songs

ALTHOUGH IT IS very common today to hear one of several translations of "Happy Birthday" in the celebration of birthdays of Spanish-speaking people, there are some specific songs authentically Latino for this occasion.

Among Mexicans and people of Mexican descent the favorite birthday song is "Las mañanitas," with many variations. In the Caribbean this is a popular version:

Felicidades, José, en tu día
que lo pases con gran alegría
muchos años de paz y armonia
¡Felicidad! ¡Felicidad¡ ¡Felicidad!

Much joy, José, on your day
May it be filled with happiness,
Long years of harmony and peace.
All happiness to you!

Las mañanitas

Estas son las mañanitas
que cantaba el Rey David
hoy por ser día de tu santo
te las cantamos a ti:

Despierta, mi bien, despierta.
Mira que ya amaneció,
ya los pajaritos cantan
la luna ya se metió.

Ya viene amaneciendo
ya la luz del día llegó.
Levántate de mañana
mira que ya amaneció.

El día en que tú naciste
nacieron las cosas bellas
nació el sol, nació la luna
y nacieron las estrellas.

Mexican Birthday Serenade

This is a birthday song,
Sung by David, the king.
Now it's your birthday,
To you we will sing:

Awake, my darling. Awake!
Little birds greet the day.
The sun is rising,
The moon drifts away.

The light of the day
Comes with the dawn.
Awake, my darling,
No time to yawn!

The day you were born
All things came to be
The sun, the moon, and stars
Shone for you and for me.

¡Qué linda está la mañana...!

¡Qué linda está la mañana
en que vengo a saludarte
venimos todos con gusto
y placer a felicitarte!

Ya las horas se adelantan,
la luna pierde su brillo,
las aves alegres cantan
entonando su estribillo.

Vengo a endulzarte el oído
con éste, mi tierno canto,
a entonar las mañanitas,
hoy que es el día de tu santo.

Yo prosigo en mis cantares,
deseando alegrar tu hogar
y con un ramo de flores
te vengo a felicitar.

How Beautiful Is This Special Day

How beautiful is this special day,
I come to greet you and to say,
We all come with great cheer
To wish you happy birthday, dear!

Hours move forward, it is morning time
The moon has now hidden its shine.
Birds are singing in trees above
Songs of joy and of love.

I come to sing sweetly in your ear
A tender melody, pure and clear
That celebrates this special day—
A day for laughter, fun, and play.

I'll continue to sing my song,
Wishing you happiness all day long.
And with this bouquet of flowers
We'll celebrate with you, every hour!

Villancicos
Christmas Carols

AMONG LATINO peoples, Christmas is not just a day or a week of festivities, but more than a month of different events, each with its own special traditions. The holiday has transcended its religous meaning to become an integral part of the culture.

The festivities begin well before Christmas Day with the *Posadas* and the building of Navitity scenes in many homes. They last until January sixth, the feast of the Epiphany, when children in most Spanish-speaking countries await the visit of the Three Wise Men, or *Los Tres Reyes Magos*: Melchor, Gaspar, and Baltasar. Children know them by their first names and leave them not only letters with requests for gifts but also water and freshly cut grass for their camels.

The *villancicos*, or Christmas carols, are an integral part of the celebrations. They may focus on the trip to Bethlehem, the birth of Jesus, or the visits of shepherds and Magi. Sometimes they are lullabies that Mary sings to her newborn babe. It may seem surprising that even within a religious context, the *villancicos* are occasionally playful. Mary and Joseph are seen as very familiar characters and the songs occasionally even mock Joseph, whose pants, in one example, are eaten by mice in the barn.

In Latin America *villancicos* often reflect local culture, particularly in the humble gifts people offer baby Jesus.

Venid, pastorcitos

Venid, pastorcitos,
venid a adorar
al Rey de los Cielos
que ha nacido ya.

Dicen los pastores
que vieron bajar
una luz del cielo
derecho al portal.

Campanitas de oro
suenan por ahí.
La Virgen María
viene por aquí.

Come, Little Shepherds

Come, little shepherds,
Come to adore
The great King of Heaven
Who is now born.

Shepherds say they saw
From the sky a light,
A light shining warmly
Into the barn so bright.

Little golden bells
Ring out clear.
The Virgin Mary
Has come here.

En el portal de Belén

En el portal de Belén
hacen fuego los pastores
para calentar al niño
que ha nacido entre las flores.

En el portal de Belén
había muchos ratones
y al bueno de San José
le han comido los calzones.

In This Barn of Bethlehem

In this barn of Bethlehem
A fire the shepherds keep
To warm the little Baby
Among the flowers, fast asleep.

In this barn of Bethlehem
There were many mice
Who ate Saint Joseph's old pants
With little mousey bites!

Villancico andino

Señora Doña María
yo vengo desde muy lejos
y a su niñito le traigo
un parcito de conejos.

Señora Doña María
yo vengo de las llanuras
y a su niñito le traigo
una frutita madura.

Señora Doña María
de muy lejos vengo aquí
y a su niñito le traigo
un gallo quiquiriquí.

Señora Doña María
deje acercarme un poquito
y sin despertar al niño
besarle los piececitos.

Señora Doña María
cogollito de alhelí
encárguele a su niñito
que no se olvide de mí.

Andean Carol

Dear Lady María,
I come from far away
To bring your little child
Some rabbits this day.

Dear Lady María,
from the plains I come
To bring your little child
Fruits, fresh and plump.

Dear Lady María,
I come from far away
To bring him a rooster.
Cockle-doodle-day!

Dear Lady María,
Allow me to get close,
And without waking the babe,
Kiss his sweet toes!

Dear Lady María,
Heart of a beautiful flower,
Please ask your blessed baby
To remember me each hour.

Esta noche es Nochebuena

Esta noche es Nochebuena
vamos al campo, hermanito,
a cortar un arbolito,
porque la noche es serena.

Los reyes y los pastores
andan siguiendo a una estrella
le cantan a Jesús niño
hijo de la Virgen bella.

Arbolito, arbolito,
campanitas te pondré
quiero que seas bonito
que al recién nacido
te voy a ofrecer.

Iremos por el camino,
caminito de Belén,
iremos porque esta noche
ha nacido el Niño Rey.

Tonight Is Christmas Night

Tonight is Christmas Night.
Oh, brother, let us go
And cut a little tree
In the country spot we know.

Kings and shepherds
All come from afar
And sing to Baby Jesus
Beneath the star.

With bells I adorn you,
Most beautiful tree,
To give to the babe
Whose birth sets us free.

To Bethlehem we go,
Following the same star,
There tonight the Child is born
Right near where we are.

Despedida
Good-bye

THE TRADITIONAL LATIN American folksingers frequently end their singing with a *copla de despedida*, a good-bye couplet. Here is one to end this book:

> Y aquí me despido.
> Vámonos andando.
> Vuelen, pajarillos,
> vuelen vigilando.

> *And here I say good-bye.*
> *Let's start our walk.*
> *Little birds, fly,*
> *Until our next talk.*

Índice

Index